Frames of Destiny

Bojana Rmandic

TANEESHA PUBLISHERS

Title : Frames of Destiny

Author : Bojana Rmandic

Edition : First (January, 2025)

ISBN : 9789348037893

Published by

TANEESHA PUBLISHERS | *A Venture by -* **PRACHI DIGITAL PUBLICATION**

Regd. Add.: 254, Khuriyakhatta No. 10, Bindukhatta,
Lalkuan, Nainital - 262402, Uttarakhand, India
Website : www.taneeshapublishers.in
E-mail : taneeshapublishers@gmail.com
Phone : +91 8454 812712, +91 8057 812712

Printed by :
Manipal Technologies Limited, Bengaluru - 560001, Karnataka

Foreword

The act of creating, whether it's through words, images, or actions, is one of the most vulnerable yet powerful things we can do. To create is to express, to share a part of ourselves with the world and to hope it resonates.

Frames of Destiny is a story about that act of creation, about the courage it takes to pursue a path that isn't always clear, and about the beauty of embracing the unknown.

Amelia Harper's journey is one of transformation. Through her lens, we see the world not only as it is, but as it can be, layered with humanity, resilience and untold stories waiting to be revealed.

Her path, however, is far from linear. Like all of us, she faces self-doubt, heartbreak, and moments of uncertainty. But it's in those challenges that she discovers the essence of who she is and what truly matters.

This book is a celebration of creativity and its ability to connect us to the world and to ourselves. It's about finding meaning not in perfection but in the raw, imperfect beauty of the journey. Amelia's story reminds us that success isn't measured by fame or accolades, but by the authenticity of the life we create.

As you turn these pages, you'll travel with Amelia to breathtaking landscapes and bustling cities, experience her triumphs and struggles and reflect on your own moments of discovery. Whether you're an artist, a dreamer or someone seeking direction, her story will resonate deeply, encouraging you to look within and embrace your own journey with courage and grace.

May Frames of Destiny inspire you to see the world differently, to cherish the quiet moments and to write your own story, one that's as meaningful and unique as the life you choose to create.

With gratitude and hope,

Bojana Rmandic

Introduction

Amelia Harper is a 30-year-old photographer whose life is as vivid and complex as the frames she captures. Deeply introspective and ambitious, she's driven by an unrelenting desire to find meaning in her work and her existence. Though she's found success in the glossy, high-pressure world of high-fashion photography, she feels hollow. The portraits she takes are stunning, technically perfect, but devoid of the authenticity and raw storytelling that first ignited her passion.

Amelia is meticulous in her craft, a perfectionist who believes that every image tells a story. She seeks to uncover beauty in places where others might only see chaos or pain. Her empathy and artistic vision fuel her creativity, but they also weigh on her, leaving her vulnerable to self-doubt. She often questions whether her work and by extension, her life truly reflects her values.

Fiercely independent, Amelia has always forged her own path, but her independence comes at a cost. She battles the ache of loneliness and a yearning for a place or person that feels like home. This duality defines her: resilient and brave in the face of adversity, yet unafraid to admit her vulnerabilities and need for connection. Her journey is one of self-discovery, as she learns to embrace imperfection, confront her fears and reconnect with the unfiltered beauty of life.

Her relationship with Hiro, eventually contributes towards her passionate journey. Hiro Takeda is an artist who embodies balance and calm, a steady counterpoint to Amelia's storm of emotions. Born and raised in Kyoto, Japan, Hiro carries with him a rich cultural heritage that informs his art and his way of life.

His work is a seamless fusion of traditional Japanese aesthetics and contemporary design, bridging the past and present in a way that feels timeless.

A man of few words, Hiro prefers to let his art speak for him. He approaches life with the same precision and mindfulness that he brings to his craft. Every stroke of his brush is intentional, every piece of his work infused with layers of meaning. His introspective nature gives him a quiet confidence, a sense of stability that draws people in without demanding attention.

Hiro's emotional intelligence is one of his greatest strengths. He has an uncanny ability to sense unspoken feelings, offering comfort or insight without the need for elaborate conversations. This makes him a grounding and calming presence in Amelia's life, especially as she wrestles with her uncertainties. He challenges her to slow down, to Savor the present moment instead of rushing toward an undefined future.

Despite his calm exterior, Hiro has faced his own share of heartbreak and loss, which have shaped his wisdom and resilience. He understands the pain of letting go and the beauty of starting anew. His openness to love, even after experiencing deep hurt, is a testament to his strength.

Perhaps it was this sense of balance, one she lacked but deeply craved, that would later draw her to Hiro and shape her journey.

In his relationship with Amelia, Hiro becomes both a muse and a partner, inspiring her to see the world and herself through a different lens. Their bond is one of mutual growth and creative energy, a space where both can explore their vulnerabilities while finding strength in one another.

Amelia and Hiro's connection is built on contrasts and harmony. She's a whirlwind of ambition and introspection, constantly searching for answers, while he's a steady force, reminding her that sometimes the answers lie in simply being. They push each other to grow. Amelia helps Hiro open up and embrace the spontaneity of life, while Hiro grounds Amelia, teaching her to find beauty in the moment rather than striving for unattainable perfection.

Together, their creative energies and shared vulnerabilities forge a bond that is both challenging and deeply fulfilling. Their partnership isn't a fairy tale, it's real, messy, and profoundly human, reflecting the very themes that Amelia seeks to capture in her art.

The story begins where Amelia harper has already spent years working in a corporate photography studio but always dreamed of traveling the world to capture untold stories. After a failed relationship and feeling stuck in her career she decided to take a leap of faith.

Amelia stood on the edge of a life she no longer recognized. A successful photographer by title, but with nothing to show for it except a wall of uninspired portraits and a handful of corporate headshots. Her passion, once a burning flame, had turned to embers under the weight of deadlines, bills and a city that demanded too much.

She stares at her camera, sitting on the cluttered desk in her tiny New York apartment. It wasn't just a tool; it was the last piece of herself that still felt alive.

"Something has to change," she whispered to the empty room.

The decision came to her as naturally as the golden hour's light spilling through her window: she would leave, not just the city, but the heartbreak, the noise, and the weight of expectations.

Her first stop? Iceland. A land as raw and untouched as she wanted to feel inside.

Chapters

Chapter 1

The Leap

Soft rain streaked the windows of my tiny New York apartment, blurring the city's relentless chaos outside. I stood there, coffee cup in hand, watching the city move below me, a chaotic rhythm of horns, footsteps and neon. Somewhere in that noise, I'd lost myself.

Outside, I had it all. People envied the glossy sheen of my life: the prestigious photography studio job, the Manhattan address, the boyfriend who looked perfect on paper. But inside? I was hollow. Every shoot felt like a transaction, every photo drained a little more of the passion I'd once had.

And then, three weeks ago, he left. Four years together, undone in a single conversation. He'd called me *"impossible to love."* Said I was too wrapped up in my dreams, too unwilling to compromise. But he was wrong about one thing, I wasn't dreaming anymore. Not really.

The rain blurred the skyline, but one thought cut through the haze: *"I can't stay here."*

That night, I sat on my bed with my laptop balanced on my knees. My coffee had gone cold, but I didn't notice. I typed the words without hesitation: *"one-way flights to Iceland."*

Iceland. I'd always been drawn to it, the volcanic landscapes, the northern lights, the way it felt untouched by time. It was everything I wasn't: wild, free, alive. Within minutes, I'd booked a ticket.

Two weeks. That's all the time I had to dismantle my life.

The days flew by in a blur of packing and goodbyes. I sold almost everything I owned, pared my life down to a suitcase, my camera and a leather-bound journal. My colleagues called me reckless. My mother phoned every hour, listing all the way this could go wrong.

But for the first time in years, I felt alive.

The morning of my flight was cold and gray, fitting for a departure. At the airport gate, I clutched my passport in one hand and my camera in the other, my heart pounding with a mixture of fear and exhilaration.

When the plane touched down in Reykjavik, the air hit me like a shock, crisp, biting, electric. The landscape stretched out before me, endless and untouched. I'd rented a tiny cottage just outside the city, perched on the edge of a volcanic field.

The stillness was unsettling at first. The silence pressed against me and I found myself questioning everything. Was I crazy? Was I running away from my problems instead of facing them?

For days, I wandered aimlessly, my camera a constant companion, and heavy in my hands. The crunch of frost beneath my boots was the only sound in the stillness. I trekked through moss-covered lava fields, stood at the edges of frozen waterfalls, stared at endless horizons. And yet, nothing I shot felt… right.

One night, the wind howled outside the cottage as I sat surrounded by prints of my photos. They stared back at me, lifeless and cold, no better than the headshots I'd left behind. Frustration welled up and I shoved the prints aside, burying my face in my hands.

"Why did I think this would work?" I muttered into the empty room.

The next morning, everything changed.

I stumbled into a small gallery in Reykjavik, drawn by the warm glow spilling onto the street. Inside, the walls were lined with breathtaking paintings, stormy skies, jagged cliffs, serene fjords. They captured the land the way I'd been trying to.

"You're not from here," a voice said behind me.

I turned to see an older woman with wild silver hair and piercing eyes.

"Is it that obvious?" I replied, forcing a smile. And I introduced myself, *" I am Amelia, Amelia harper."*

"You look lost, Amelia" she said simply. *"What are you searching for?"*

I hesitated. *"I don't know. Myself, maybe? Inspiration?"*

She studied me for a moment, then nodded. *"Stop looking so hard. Let the land speak to you. Follow your lens and the truth will come."*

Her words lingered like a melody I couldn't shake, guiding me in ways I didn't yet understand . Over the next few days, I let go of my expectations. I stopped trying to find the shot and started noticing the small things: the way frost laced the grass in delicate patterns, the way light spilled over the mountains, the joy of a child chasing a puffin along the shore.

Slowly, my camera began to feel like an extension of me again.

Two weeks later, I stood on a black sand beach, the northern lights erupting across the sky in waves of green and purple. I raised my camera, my breath catching.

For the first time in years, something stirred deep within me, a joy, I thought I'd lost forever, rising like the lights above.

The shutter clicked, and I smiled. This was just the beginning.

Chapter 2
Iceland's Reflection

The next morning, I woke to silence, not the comforting kind, but the kind that pressed against my ears and made my heart race. The cottage was steeped in darkness, except for the faint silver glow of the moon slicing through the curtains. I glanced at the clock: 4:00 AM. Another restless night, another tangle of unanswered questions. Sleep was becoming a distant luxury.

The quiet I had once craved now felt suffocating, heavy and unrelenting, as if the stillness itself was conspiring to unearth every buried thought and regret. Back in New York, the constant hum of the city had been my escape, a way to drown out the noise in my own head. But here, in this untouched, desolate land, there was no hiding. The solitude filled every corner, daring me to face parts of myself I wasn't ready to meet.

By sunrise, I was out the door, camera slung over my shoulder. The sharp, cold air bit my cheeks, cutting through the layers I'd hastily thrown on. There was a metallic tang to the breeze, a reminder of the volcanic terrain beneath my feet. My boots sank into the spongy moss as I trudged forward, unsure of my destination but desperate to feel something other than this gnawing doubt.

Ahead, I spotted it: a waterfall crashing down from jagged rocks, its icy spray catching the first rays of morning light. The roar was deafening, drowning out the thoughts swirling in my head. I set up my tripod, carefully framing the shot. Adjusting the focus, tweaking the exposure. But no matter how I composed the image, it felt wrong, flat, lifeless, like it was mocking me.

Frustration surged. My fingers tightened around the camera strap before I let it fall to my side. I sank onto a nearby rock, the cold biting through my coat as tears pricked the corners of my eyes. I buried my face in my hands, my breath coming out in short, visible puffs. What was I thinking? Leaving New York, walking away from stability, from everything I knew, it felt reckless now, like a bet I'd already lost.

"Beautiful, isn't it?"

I hadn't heard her approach. My heart jumped, and I turned to see. A woman stood a few feet away, wrapped in a thick wool coat. Her silver hair shimmered in the sunlight, her pale blue eyes holding a quiet intensity that seemed to see right through me.

"It is," I said softly, my voice barely audible over the roar of the waterfall.

She stepped closer, her boots crunching on the frost-covered ground. *"I've been coming here for years. This place has a way of showing you who you are if you're willing to look."*

I didn't know how to respond, so I didn't.

Her gaze shifted to the camera hanging from my shoulder. *"So, ... You're a photographer?"*

I nodded. *"I am. Or... I was. Lately, I'm not so sure."*

She studied me for a long moment, her expression unreadable. Then, with a small smile, she said, *"You're searching too hard. Stop trying to find the perfect picture. Let the picture find you."*

Before I could ask what she meant, she turned and walked away, her figure disappearing into the mist rising from the waterfall. I sat there for a long time, replaying her words in my mind. Her words echoed the advice of the woman I'd met a few days earlier, as if the land itself was conspiring to remind me not to give up, not to try so hard.

The next morning, I decided to take her advice. I left the tripod behind and walked out with just my camera in hand, no agenda, no expectations. I let my feet guide me, wandering without purpose or pressure.

For the first time, I began to notice the little things. The way frost clung to the edges of leaves, glinting like shards of glass in the sunlight. The shadows of clouds racing across the plains, chasing each other over the endless horizon. The intricate patterns etched into the lava rock beneath my boots, as if an unseen artist had carved the earth itself.

I stopped thinking about composition. Instead, I started feeling, letting the land speak to me rather than forcing it into the confines of my lens.

By the time I returned to the cottage that evening, my cheeks were flushed from the cold and my hands were trembling not from exhaustion, but from something else, something I hadn't felt in months.

Excitement.

I uploaded the photos to my laptop, leaning forward as the screen filled with image after image. They weren't perfect. Some were overexposed, others blurred. But they were real.

My breath caught as I stared at the raw, unpolished beauty of what I had captured. For the first time in what felt like forever, something deep within me flickered to life, a small but unmistakable spark.

Maybe, just maybe, I hadn't lost myself after all.

Chapter 3
Italy's colors

The heat enveloped me as I stepped off the train in Florence, heavy and humid, wrapping around me like a living thing. It was both stifling and intoxicating. The air was thick with the aroma of stone-baked bread, roasted coffee, and the faint metallic tang of cobblestones worn smooth by centuries of footsteps. Unlike Iceland, with its vast, empty landscapes, Italy felt alive, buzzing with energy in every corner.

I had rented a small room above a bakery in the heart of the city. It wasn't much, just a bed, a desk and a single window overlooking a narrow street, but it felt vibrant in a way my New York apartment never had. Every morning, the soft hum of voices and the aroma of freshly baked focaccia drifted through the walls, pulling me into a rhythm that felt foreign yet comforting.

The first days in Florence were a whirlwind of sensory overload. I wandered through the crowded piazzas, my camera ever-present, capturing the chaos and charm of the city. Children chased pigeons through cobblestone squares, their laughter echoing like church bells. Elderly couples shared gelato, their smiles radiant like music. Street performers spun tales for tourists, their voices rising above the clinking of espresso cups and the rhythmic murmur of conversation.

The markets were a feast for the senses. Wooden crates overflowed with the brightest oranges, reds, and greens I'd ever seen, peppers, tomatoes, lemons all so vibrant they seemed painted. I snapped photo after photo, trying to catch the life packed in every corner. But even as I captured the beauty, I felt like something was missing.

That missing piece found me one quiet evening, as the sun melted into the horizon. I followed the faint strains of music through Florence's labyrinthine streets until I stumbled upon a small dimly lit piazza.

In the piazza's fading light, a man stood with a weathered guitar, his eyes closed as he played. His hands strumming the guitar with a kind of devotion that made the air around him hum. His voice carried a melody I couldn't understand, yet it filled the air like an incantation, wrapping itself around the small crowd and sinking into my chest.

A small crowd had gathered, the kind that blends into the background when something extraordinary is unfolding. No one noticed as I raised my camera. I snapped a photo, then another, capturing him mid-song. I could feel it, this wasn't just another picture. It was alive, electric.

The next day, while wandering the sun-dappled streets of Florence, I came across a tiny gallery tucked away in a quiet corner. The wooden sign above the door was faded, its painted letters barely legible. Inside, an older man with salt-and-pepper hair was carefully arranging a collection of local art.

He looked up as I entered, his eyes brightening when he saw the camera hanging around my neck.

"You're a photographer?" he asked in Italian accented English.

I hesitated. *"Yes... I mean, I'm trying to be."*

He smiled and motioned for me to sit. *"Show me your work."*

For a moment, I froze. My fingers hovered over my camera, doubt stressing at me. But then I thought of the man with the guitar, the way his song had filled that piazza. I pulled up the photo and handed the camera to him.

Marco that was his name, leaned forward, his eyes narrowing as he studied the images, each swipe of his fingers feeling like an eternity. I held my breath, bracing for judgement, unsure whether I wanted him to speak or remain silent forever.

When he finally looked up, there was a smile tugging at the corners of his mouth.

"These," he said, pointing to a few of the images, *"are not just pictures. They are stories. You see the world differently."*

Something in me cracked open. My heart raced. *"Thank you,"* I murmured, barely trusting my voice.

Marco leaned back in his chair, his expression thoughtful. *"I want to feature your work in my gallery. It's not much, just a small space, but I think people will love it."*

I stared at him, unsure if I had heard correctly. *"Really?"*

He nodded. *"Yes. But only if you promise me one thing."*

"What's that?" I asked, my voice tinged with a mix of anxiety and anticipation.

"Keep photographing the truth. That's what makes your work powerful." He smiled and said goodbye.

The words lingered, settling into a place I hadn't realized was empty. For the first time in what felt like forever, I wasn't just taking pictures, I was creating something, with color, people and sounds that had awakened something inside me. I felt like real.

For the first time, I felt like I was on the right path.

Chapter 4

India's Chaos and Clarity

I was greeted by a heavy, suffocating heat wave as I stepped out of the Delhi airport and into chaos. The air was filled with an intoxicating mixture of spices, exhaust fumes and the faint sweetness of something unplaceable. The streets pulsed with life, every corner alive with movement and sound. Rickshaws drifted through traffic like dancers in an unchoreographed routine, vendors shouted over one another and people flowed in currents that seemed both chaotic and effortless.

My heart pounded in my chest. Iceland had been quiet, almost meditative. Italy, vibrant but familiar. But India? India was something else entirely, an assault on the senses, raw, loud, and overwhelming. It wasn't what I'd imagined; it was far more.

I'd come here with a vague plan: to photograph the intricacies of everyday life. But as I stepped into the streets, camera in hand, I realized how unprepared I was. The city didn't exist; it breathed, it demanded to be seen.

The first days in Delhi were disorienting. The city didn't just exist, it breathed, throbbed, demanded to be noticed. I wandered through the crowded bazaars, camera slung awkwardly over my shoulder, unsure when or if I should even use it. The stalls were an explosion of color, shimmering saris draped like waterfalls, jewellery glinting like trapped sunlight, and spices piled high in reds, golds, and deep oranges.

The air was a discord of voices bargaining, the metallic clang of pots and the distant, melodic call to prayer. Every corner offered a scene more vivid than the last, but something held me back. Fear, maybe. The fear of being an intruder in a world that wasn't mine.

It wasn't until the third day that I raised my camera. I saw her sitting on the edge of a stall, weaving marigolds into garlands. Her hands moved deftly, knotting each flower with a precision that seemed effortless. When she glanced up, her eyes met mine and something unspoken passed between us, a quiet understanding that needed no words. Her smile unfolded slowly, warm and crinkled. A smile that reached all the way to her soul, as she had been waiting for this moment.

I lifted my camera, my hands trembling slightly, and clicked.

That smile changed something inside me. With each frame I captured, the fear loosened its grip. I realized that these moments, the smile of a stranger, the simple act of weaving marigolds, were bridge between worlds.

A week later, I found myself in a small village in Rajasthan. The air was cooler here, carrying the earthy scent of clay mixed with the faint sweetness of blooming jasmine. I'd been invited by a local NGO to document the lives of women artisans, craftswomen whose hands transformed the ordinary into something extraordinary.

One woman, Priya, caught my eye immediately. Her hands, worn and calloused, moved with steady rhythm of someone who had spent years perfecting the craft. Each stroke of the brush seemed to carry a story, etched in the lines of her fingers and the patterns she painted onto a vase. Her eyes carried a sadness that spoke of loss, but behind it was a fierce determination.

Through a translator, I learned her story. Priya's husband had passed away years ago, leaving her to provide for their three children on her own. The crafts she created weren't just beautiful, they were her lifeline.

"May I take a picture of you?" I asked gently.

She hesitated, her fingers pausing mid-stroke. Then she nodded. *"If it helps people see us, see what we do, then yes,"* she said softly in Hindi.

I spent hours with Priya and the other women, capturing their hands at work, their faces bent in concentration, the stories etched into their lives. The photos I took were unlike anything I'd ever captured before. They weren't just images, they were truths. Raw, intimate, human truths that felt like they'd been waiting for me to find them.

One evening, as the sun dipped below the horizon, I sat with Priya on the steps of her small home. The village had grown quiet, the air cool and still.

"Why do you take photos?" Priya asked, her voice breaking the silence.

I thought for a moment, letting the question settle. *"Because it's the only way I know how to understand the world,"* I said finally. *"And sometimes, it's the only way I can understand myself."*

She nodded, her expression soft. *"Yes. That is why I paint."*

We sat there together, two women who didn't speak the same language but shared something deeper, a need to create, to express, to be seen.

That night, I uploaded the day's photos to my laptop. As the images filled the screen, a lump rose in my throat. These weren't just pictures. They were moments. Proof of beauty and resilience in places so many would overlook.

One photo stood out: Priya, her hands stained with paint, her eyes steady and defiant. It was a portrait of strength, of survival.

A week later, that photo went viral.

The NGO used it in a campaign to raise awareness about the artisans' work and the response was overwhelming. Donations poured in and orders began arriving from across the globe.

I received dozens of messages, but one stood out: *"Your photos remind us that the world is full of stories waiting to be told. Thank you for telling them."*

I sat back in my chair, tears welling in my eyes. After an exceedingly long time, I felt like my work mattered.

As I prepared to leave India, I reflected on everything the country had given me. Iceland had taught me to embrace stillness. Italy had reignited my passion. And India? India had shown me the power of connection, of seeing and being seen. It has shown me that every face, every gesture, every moment held a story waiting to be told.

As the train sped through the countryside, the fields blurred into streaks of green and gold, I realized that photography wasn't just my craft, it was my way of bearing witness, of giving voice to the unnoticed beauty in the world. My story was just beginning, and so were theirs.

I wasn't just a photographer anymore. I was a storyteller.

My camera rested in my lap; my bags tucked safely at my feet. And then, I felt a sense of clarity. And my story was just beginning.

Chapter 5

Japan's Harmony

The cherry blossoms were just beginning to bloom when I arrived in Kyoto. The city unfolded before me like a dream, quiet yet alive, bustling yet serene. After the vibrant chaos of India, Japan felt like a whispered promise of peace, a place where life moved with deliberate grace. Each step along its quiet streets felt like shedding a layer of the chaos I had carried with me.

Walking through the streets was like stepping into a painting, soft hues of pink and green blending with the timeless elegance of wooden bridges. Temples rose from lush green hills, their pagodas reaching toward the sky as if in conversation with the heavens. Cherry blossoms lined the pathways, their delicate petals drifting to the ground like soft pink snow. The air carried a faint, soothing mix of incense and rain-soaked earth, and with each breath, I felt my chest loosen.

I exhaled deeply, the tension I hadn't realized I was holding releasing with the breeze. After weeks of chasing stories and frames, this stillness was what I hadn't known I needed.

My days in Kyoto began before sunrise. The city seemed to wake slowly, almost reverently and I found myself matching its rhythm. I would walk to the nearest temple in the cool, gray light of dawn, my camera slung over my shoulder but forgotten as I took in the calm.

There were no honking horns or shouting vendors here. Instead, the air was filled with the hum of bicycles passing quietly, the rustle of kimono-clad women and the rhythmic sound of bamboo fountains filling and emptying with water.

For hours, I would lose myself in the details: the soft pink of cherry blossoms against the weathered wood of temple gates, the intricate patterns of koi fish gliding through crystal-clear ponds, the way light filtered through shoji screens in a teahouse. For the first time, I started to see beauty in the spaces in between, the pauses, the silences, the breaths between moments.

One afternoon, while wandering through the Arashiyama Bamboo Grove, I noticed a man sitting cross-legged on a stone bench, sketching. His pencil moved with slow, deliberate precision; his gaze focused entirely on his work.

I hesitated, unsure whether to interrupt. But there was something about the way he worked that reminded me of myself, completely absorbed, completely present. Instinctively, I raised my camera and clicked. The sound of the shutter broke the stillness, and the man looked up, startled.

Our eyes met, and he smiled. *"You caught me,"* he said, his English flawless.

"Sorry," I said quickly, lowering my camera. *"I didn't mean to interrupt."*

"You didn't." He closed his sketchpad with deliberate care and stood, extending a hand. *"I'm Hiro. And you?"*

"Amelia," I replied, shaking his hand. *"What are you sketching?"*

He held up the pad, revealing an intricate drawing of the bamboo grove. Every detail was rendered with a precision and care that took my breath away.

"It's beautiful," I said sincerely.

"Thank you," he replied. *"And you? What are you capturing?"*

I smiled, lifting my camera slightly. *"The same thing, I guess. Just... in an unusual way."*

He laughed softly and before I knew it, we were walking through the grove together, talking about art, storytelling, and the beauty of simplicity. Hiro told me he was an architect specializing in traditional Japanese design. His work, like mine, was rooted in a love of detail and a desire to tell stories.

Over the next week, Hiro showed me parts of Kyoto I never would have found on my own. He took me to a hidden garden behind an unexceptional teahouse, a tiny bookstore filled with handmade journals, and a quiet stretch of the Kamo River where fireflies danced at night.

There was something about Hiro that drew me in, not just his kindness, but the way he saw the world. He noticed the trivial things, the in-between moments, with the same quiet reverence I was learning to embrace.

Hiro's way of seeing the world through lines, balance, and harmony of tradition and modernity began to influence my photography. I found myself lingering on the spaces between moments, the quiet simplicity I might have overlooked before.

One evening, as we sat by the river, the fireflies' light flickering like tiny stars, he turned to me. *"Why do you travel, Amelia?"*

The question lingered in the air, simple yet profound. I looked out at the water, its ripples catching the fireflies' glow, letting the sound of it fill the silence before answering. *"I guess... I'm searching for something,"* I said finally. *"Or maybe I'm searching for myself."*

Hiro nodded thoughtfully. *"And have you found it?"*

I watched the fireflies for a moment longer before answering. *"I think I'm starting to,"* I said softly.

When it was time to leave Kyoto, a pang of sadness hit me that I hadn't expected. As I stood on the train platform, Hiro smiled at me, his expression calm and steady.

"Your story isn't finished," he said. *"And neither is mine. Maybe our paths will cross again."*

I nodded, his words settling deep inside me as I boarded the train. Through the window, I watched Kyoto fade into the distance, the temples, the cherry blossoms, and Hiro standing quietly on the platform.

I had come to Japan searching for balance, but I was leaving with something far more valuable. Life, like photography, is about focus. Sometimes, you have to step back, adjust the lens, and let the picture come into view.

As the train sped through the countryside, the fields blurred into streaks of green and pink. Somewhere in the quiet spaces between my past and my future, I felt something I hadn't in a long time.

Peace.

Leaving Japan stayed with me longer than I expected. As I travelled from Tokyo to other parts of Asia, then back to Europe, Hiro's memory lingered, woven into the fabric of my days. The quiet conversations by the river, the way his sketches mirrored my photographs, it all felt like pieces of a puzzle I hadn't realized was incomplete.

But one thing I had learned during this journey was that my life wasn't about waiting for others to fill the gaps. It was about creating my own story, one frame at a time.

As my journey continued, each destination left its mark, shaping me in ways I hadn't anticipated. By the time I returned to New York, the city felt both familiar and transformed, as though I was seeing it with new eyes.

The city buzzed with its usual frenetic energy, the rush of people, the blare of taxi horns, the hum of lights that never dimmed. But this time, it felt different. I felt different. Calmer, more grounded, like the noise couldn't shake me anymore.

My photographs from my travels had gained unexpected attention. The series from India, especially, had been picked up by a major magazine, which had led to an invitation to exhibit at one of New York's most prestigious galleries.

The opening night was just days away. I poured myself into preparing, arranging the prints, writing captions, obsessing over the details. But no matter how much I threw myself into the work, I couldn't shake the feeling that something or someone was missing.

The gallery buzzed with life on opening night. Friends, critics, and strangers alike filled the space, their murmurs of admiration weaving through the air. I stood off to the side, overwhelmed by the crowd but proud of what I had created.

The exhibition had come together just as I'd envisioned: each series representing a chapter of my journey. Stories of Iceland's stillness, Italy's vibrance, India's resilience, and finally Japan's harmony.

As I explained my work to a group of journalists, I glanced toward the entrance and froze.

Hiro stood in the doorway, a small bouquet of cherry blossoms in his hands. He looked slightly out of place among the crowd, but his warm smile was unmistakable.

I excused myself and crossed the room, my heart pounding.

"Hiro," I said, my voice catching somewhere between surprise and joy. *"What are you doing here?"*

"I couldn't miss this," he said, holding out the bouquet. *"Your photos, they're incredible. They tell a story only you could tell."*

Tears pricked my eyes as I took the flowers. *"Thank you,"* I said softly. *"It means a lot that you're here."*

Later that night, as the gallery emptied and the city began to quiet, Hiro and I sat together on a bench outside. The lights of New York twinkled like fireflies, casting a warm glow over the moment.

"I wasn't sure I'd ever see you again," I admitted, breaking the silence.

Hiro turned to me, his smile steady and reassuring. *"I told you; our stories aren't finished. And I have a feeling they're more connected than we realized."*

I looked at him, his words settling into my chest like the steady rhythm of a heartbeat. For the first time, I didn't just see the end of my journey, I saw the threads of a new beginning, woven with the same quiet harmony I had come to cherish in Japan.

As the city buzzed faintly around us, I realized that this too was part of the story, I'd been searching for all along.

Chapter 6
The Spotlight

I stood in front of the gallery window, staring at the sign bearing my name. *Amelia Carter: A World Unseen*. My stomach fluttered with a mix of pride and nerves. This wasn't just an exhibition; it was my story. Every frame inside told a piece of the journey I had taken across continents, the lessons I had learned, the lives I had captured.

The gallery had offered me this solo exhibition after seeing my work from India, and since then, the buzz had only grown. Critics were calling me the *"Voice of modern humanity,"* and collectors were already lining up to buy prints. It was everything I'd dreamt of, everything I had worked for and yet, as the opening night drew closer, I couldn't help but wonder: was I truly ready for the world to see me this way?

The evening began with a speech by the gallery director, a charismatic woman who spoke about my work as if she had lived each of those moments with me.

"Amelia Carter's work is more than photography," she said, her voice carrying across the crowded space. *"It is a bridge between cultures, a lens through which we see not only the world but also ourselves. Her work captures more than just beauty, it captures the soul of every place she's been and every person she's met. Amelia Carter is not just a photographer; she is a storyteller."*

The applause erupted, filling the room. My heart raced as I stepped forward, champagne glass in my hand, my palms damp with nerves.

As I faced the crowd, I realized something, I wasn't the same woman who had boarded a plane to Iceland all those months ago.

I had been searching back then, unsure of myself, unsure of my path. Now, I was stronger. Braver. I felt ready not just to stand in front of this crowd, but to own my vision and the stories I was telling.

As I took the microphone, I felt the weight of the crowd's gaze. But instead of fear, I felt a quiet resolve. This was my story, and I was ready to share it.

"Thank you," I began, my voice steadier than I expected. *"This exhibition is more than just photographs to me. It's a reflection of the lessons I've learned and the people who have shaped my journey. Every image here is a story of resilience, connection, and the beauty of imperfection. And I'm so grateful to share these stories with you tonight."*

The crowd dispersed and the gallery hummed with life. Friends, collectors, and journalists moved through the space, their murmured conversations weaving together like music.

I found myself swept into a blur of conversations, answering questions about my travels, my process and the moments that had shaped the photographs.

A well-known art critic approached me, his eyes bright with admiration. *"You've managed to capture something rare,"* he said.

"Your work doesn't just show the world, it feels it. I'd love to feature you in an upcoming issue of Art Now."

I blinked, struggling to process his words. Art Now. It felt surreal. *"I'd be honoured,"* I said, my voice catching slightly.

By the end of the evening, nearly half of my prints had sold. I had received invitations to exhibit in Paris, London, and Tokyo. The buzz, the praise, the opportunities, it was everything for which I had worked.

Back in my apartment that night, I sat by the window, staring out at the city lights stretching endlessly into the night. The thrill of the evening still buzzed in my veins, but as the silence wrapped around me, I felt something else.

Gratitude.

My phone buzzed, pulling me from my thoughts. It was a text from Hiro.

"Congratulations. Tonight was only the beginning. You've earned every moment of this."

I smiled, my heart full. Hiro's presence at the gallery had been grounding, a reminder of what truly mattered. The success, the acclaim, it was exhilarating. But it was the connections I'd made, the stories I'd captured and shared, that made it all meaningful.

The next few months felt like a whirlwind. My work was featured in major publications, and I was invited to speak at art and photography conferences around the world.

But no matter how far I climbed, I never lost sight of what had brought me here, the stories.

The success had given me a platform, and I wanted to use it to lift others. I started a foundation to support young photographers from underrepresented backgrounds, offering mentorship and funding for travel-based projects, offering them a chance to tell their own stories, to see and share the world through their unique lenses. I wanted others to experience the world the way I had. To feel its chaos, its harmony, its heartbreak, and its hope.

One evening, as I prepared for my first Paris exhibition, my phone rang. Hiro's name lit up the screen, and I answered with a smile.

"You've become quite the star," he teased, his voice warm and familiar.

I laughed. *"I couldn't have done it without you."*

"Well," he said, his voice softening, *"Paris is a city for dreamers. And I think you'll find me there in a few weeks. Maybe we can dream together."*

My heart skipped a beat. For the first time in my life, I felt a sense of wholeness, a career I'd fought so hard to build and the quiet promise of a love I'd only just begun to hope for.

As I sat in the quiet of my apartment, the city's hum faintly rising in the distance, I realized that this moment, this life I was creating, wasn't the end of my journey.

It was the beginning of something far greater.

Chapter 7

Paris and Passion

I stepped onto the cobblestone streets of Paris, and for a moment, I couldn't breathe. Paris wasn't just another destination, it was a dream, one I had carried with me since the day I first picked up a camera. The city hummed with life and possibility, its golden light spilling across the Seine, casting long, elegant shadows that danced on the water's surface.

The exhibition at the gallery was only days away, but I felt strangely calm. Maybe it was the city's rhythm, or maybe it was knowing that Hiro would be arriving tomorrow. It had been months since New York, but our conversations-long, meandering and unexpectedly intimate, had revealed layers of connection I hadn't dared to hope for.

Hiro arrived on a quiet morning, stepping into the café where I waited. My coffee sat untouched, my fingers tracing absent patterns on the table. When our eyes met, the world seemed to blur, like the moment before a photograph comes into focus. A wave of warmth swept over me. His familiar presence, the way he carried himself with quiet confidence, felt like a piece of home I hadn't realized been missing.

"You're here," I said softly, standing to greet him.

He smiled, setting his bag down. *"Did you think I'd miss Paris?"*

We spent the day wandering through the city, his presence grounding me in a way I hadn't realized I needed. I took him to my favourite spots, the bookshelves of Shakespeare and Company, the bridges over the Seine, the quiet bistro tucked away from the chaos of tourists.

As we strolled along the riverbank, the breeze carrying the scent of freshly baked bread, I found myself watching him as much as the city. Hiro had a way of observing everything, his eyes lingering on the textures of the walls, the way light filtered through the trees.

As the sun dipped below the Parisian skyline, Hiro accompanied me to the gallery. Together we adjusted the lighting on the photographs, his quiet suggestions transforming each frame with a subtle brilliance.

When we reached the series, I had taken in Japan, he paused, studying each frame with a thoughtful expression.

"Your work is incredible," he said finally, his voice quiet but certain. *"But it's more than that. It's honest. It's... you."*

I turned to him, my heart catching in my chest. There was something in his voice, something that reached past the words and settled deep within me.

The night before the exhibition, Hiro invited me to his rented apartment. It was a small, cozy space overlooking the city, its windows thrown open to let in the cool Parisian breeze.

He cooked for me, a simple Japanese dish that filled the room with warmth and the scent of miso and ginger. We ate on the balcony, the Eiffel Tower glittering in the distance like something out of a dream.

"I've missed this," he said, his voice low.

"Missed what?" I asked, setting my glass down.

"Sharing quiet moments with you." His eyes met mine and I felt the pull between us, the unspoken connection we had danced around for months.

His hand brushed against mine, and the space between us seemed to dissolve. *"Hiro..."* I began, my voice barely a whisper. But then he leaned closer, his lips meeting mine in a kiss that was soft, yet certain, filled with the weight of all the words we hadn't spoken. The city, the gallery, the uncertainty of tomorrow, all seemed to fall away, leaving only us and the quiet magic of this moment and Paris.

That night, as we lay together in the soft glow of the city lights, Hiro traced his fingers along my arm, his touch feather-light.

"Do you ever wonder what's next?" he asked, his voice barely more than a whisper.

"All the time," I admitted. *"But for the first time, I'm okay not knowing. It feels like... everything is falling into place."*

He smiled, brushing a strand of hair from my face. *"You're incredible, Amelia. You've built a life full of meaning. And I... I want to be part of it."*

My chest tightened, tears pricking at the corners of my eyes. *"You already are,"* I said, my voice trembling.

When the evening of the exhibition arrived, the gallery was alive with energy, every corner buzzing with anticipation and admiration. Admirers filled the space, their voices rising and falling in waves of conversation. I stood in the centre, the center of attention, and yet I didn't feel overwhelmed.

My eyes scanned the crowd until they landed on Hiro. He wasn't mingling or engaging with the others, he was watching me. His expression was quiet and filled with pride.

Paris had given me more than I ever dreamed: clarity, passion, and a quiet reminder that the most beautiful stories often unfold in ways we cannot plan. As I stood there, Hiro's steady gaze grounding me, I realized that my journey wasn't just about the places I'd seen or the photos I'd taken, it was about the connections, the love, and the courage to embrace the unexpected.

Chapter 8

Shadows in the Spotlight

Paris had been perfect, too perfect, I realized as I stepped off the plane in New York a week later. The city's energy greeted me with its familiar chaos a sharp contrast to the dreamlike serenity I had left behind.

I was back to my home, but instead of excitement, I felt the weight of it pressing down on me. The glittering skyline that had once inspired me now felt like a cage. Deadlines loomed, emails piled up and the press's fascination with my work was beginning to shift to scrutiny.

And Hiro? He had stayed behind in Paris to finish a project of his own. We had promised to talk every day, to bridge the distance with calls and messages. But I was learning that distance has a way of stretching promises thin, fraying them at the edges until they feel like they might snap.

Life in New York was a whirlwind, a relentless storm of expectations that left little room to breathe. A constant tug-of-war between opportunity and exhaustion.

The opportunities I had once dreamed of were pouring in, high-profile collaborations, campaigns with luxury brands, interviews with glossy magazines. But with every opportunity came pressure. A fashion house wanted me to shoot a campaign that felt glossy and detached, completely at odds with the authenticity I had worked so hard to maintain.

"Your rise has been... unusually fast," an editor hinted during a meeting, her tone dripping with skepticism. *"Do you think you'll be able to sustain it?"*

Her words lingered, striking a nerve I hadn't realized was exposed. I had always prided myself on seeing the humanity in my subject, but had I let the spotlight blind me to their stories? Was I turning into the kind of artist I'd once sworn I'd never become?

The campaigns felt sterile, their glossy perfection clashing with the raw, unfiltered stories I had worked so hard to tell. Was this what success looked like? A slow compromise of everything I believed in.

Late one night, after another gruelling day, I called Hiro. The exhaustion was clear in my voice as I confessed, *"Sometimes I feel like I'm losing control. Like everything I've worked for is slipping away."*

"You're not losing anything," he said, his voice calm and steady, the way it always was. *"You're just evolving. It's part of the process."*

But there was something distant in his tone, something I didn't want to confront. I pushed it aside, not wanting to add more weight to an already unsteady plate.

The tension between us grew as weeks turned into months. My schedule became relentless, leaving little time for anything else. And Hiro's messages became shorter, his calls less frequent.

One evening, as I scrolled through social media, a photo stopped me cold. It was Hiro at a Parisian event, standing close to a woman I didn't recognize. My chest tightened as I stared at the photo. I wanted to believe it was nothing, just an innocent moment, but old insecurities bubbled to the surface, whispering doubts I thought I'd left behind.

When we finally spoke, the words tumbled out before I could stop them. *"Who was she?"*

He sighed, the sound heavy over the phone. *"A colleague. Nothing more. Amelia, you know me better than that."*

"I do," I said, my voice trembling. *"But sometimes it feels like you're slipping away."*

"And sometimes," he countered, his voice sharper than I'd ever heard it, *"it feels like there's no room for me in your life anymore."*

His words hit me like a slap. I wanted to argue, to tell him he was wrong, but deep down, I knew there was truth in what he was saying.

I threw myself into my work, hoping it would drown out the turmoil in my personal life. The foundation I had started for young photographers was gaining traction, but even that came with its own challenges.

"You've been everywhere," one of the artists I mentored said to me, frustration evident in her voice. *"But do you really see the people you photograph? Or are they just subjects to you?"*

Her words haunted me. Had I lost sight of why I started this journey in the first place?

One cold evening, as I walked home from my studio, my phone buzzed. Hiro's name lit up the screen.

"Amelia," he began, his voice softer than it had been in weeks. *"I'm sorry. For the distance, for the arguments. I never meant to hurt you."*

Tears slipped down my cheeks before I could stop them. *"I'm sorry, too,"* I said, my voice trembling. *"I've been so consumed by everything, by the fear of failing, of losing myself."*

There was a long pause before he spoke again. *"Come back to Paris,"* he said softly, his voice a plea and a promise all at once. *"Not forever. Just for a little while. Let's find our way back to each other."* The vulnerability in his words broke through walls I had built.

The thought of stepping away, of seeing Hiro again, was tempting. But commitments in New York loomed, each one shouting for my attention.

"I'll think about it," I said, though my heart had already decided. As I packed my bags, a quiet hope began to bloom in my chest. Paris had given me clarity once before maybe it could do so again. Maybe it could remind me of the parts of myself I'd lost in the chaos.

A week later, I was back in Paris. Hiro met me at the airport. And the moment we embraced, the tension that had followed me for months seemed to melt away.

Our time together wasn't perfect. We had long, difficult conversations about our fears and insecurities. We aired the doubts and wounds we had both been carrying. But in between, there were moments of laughter, of connection, of joy, the kind that reminded me of why I had fallen for him in the first place.

One night, as we walked along the Seine, the city lights shimmering on the water, Hiro stopped and turned to me.

"You once told me you were searching for something," he said. *"Do you think you've found it?"*

I looked out at the river, the soft murmur of the city wrapping around us. *"I think I'm still searching,"* I admitted. *"But I know I'm closer than I've ever been."*

Hiro smiled, his hand brushing against mine before taking it fully. *"Then let's keep searching. Together."* His words felt like a lifeline, anchoring me in the present while opening the door to the future. Now the path ahead didn't feel o uncertain, it felt full of possibility.

Chapter 9

The Crossroads

My return to Paris was supposed to be temporary, a brief reprieve to catch my breath. But with each passing day, I felt more at peace. Hiro was here, steady, present and our connection had reignited in ways that both comforted and surprised me.

And yet, something tugged at the edges of my happiness, a quiet reminder that life outside our little bubble was still waiting for me.

The foundation was flourishing, my latest photo series was being hailed as groundbreaking, and the art scene in New York had started to notice my absence. For the first time in my life, I felt truly torn, caught between my personal desires and the relentless pull of my professional dreams.

One evening, Hiro took me to an intimate exhibition by a photographer I'd admired for years. The gallery was small, tucked away on a quiet Parisian Street.

The photographs were raw and unfiltered, capturing the struggles and joys of marginalized communities. I couldn't look away, entranced by the artist's unapologetic approach. But as I lingered in front of one image, a child laughing amidst rubble, a gnawing discomfort began to creep in.

"Do you ever feel like you've sold out?" I asked Hiro suddenly. *"I mean… all these commercial shoots. Sometimes, it feels like my work is just about the paycheck now."*

Hiro looked at me thoughtfully, his gaze steady. *"You've always been true to yourself, Amelia. Your work has meaning, even if it's not always in the places you expect. But if you feel like you're losing that, it's okay to step back. No one's forcing you to keep going at this pace."*

His words weighed heavily on me. I started to wonder if the fame I had worked so hard for was worth the cost. Was it worth losing myself in the process?

A few days later, the question came to a head.

An offer arrived, an exclusive contract with a major fashion brand. It was everything of which I had dreamed. The kind of opportunity that would cement my place among the top photographers in the world.

And yet, as I stared at the contract in my hands, something inside me recoiled. The glossy pages seemed to reflect a version of myself I didn't recognize. Was I chasing the art I loved, or was I chasing approval?

"Is this what I want?" I whispered aloud, my voice barely audible.

Hiro noticed my distant mood. *"You don't have to say yes,"* he said gently, taking my hand. *"You've already built a life full of meaning, Amelia. This doesn't define you. Don't let anyone, not even yourself, make you forget that."*

The pressure to accept stressed me. The financial security, the recognition, any artist would have killed for this chance. But a part of me longed for something simpler.

That night, I lay awake, my mind racing. I thought about the moments that had brought me joy, walking through the streets of India, watching the northern lights in Iceland, sharing stories with strangers who didn't care who I was or what I did.

Those were the moments that made me feel alive. *"Was fame really the answer? Or was it just another form of loneliness, wrapped in a shiny package?"* I asked myself.

The next morning, as I prepared to leave for the photoshoot with the fashion brand, Hiro stopped me.

"Whatever you decide, I want you to know I'll support you," he said, his voice soft but certain. *"But I want you to be honest with yourself. What's truly in your heart?"*

I swallowed hard. The weight of his words felt like a mountain. Who was I without the camera, without the accolades and spotlight?

Standing at the crossroads of ambition and authenticity, I realized that the path forward wasn't just about choosing one or the other. It was about carving a new road, one that honored both my values and my dreams.

By midday, I had made my decision.

I cancelled the photoshoot. I called my manager and told her I needed to take a step back, for a while, at least. The offer from the fashion brand was put on hold and instead, I poured myself into the foundation.

I began mentoring young photographers again, walking alongside them as they discovered their voices. I took long walks through Paris, letting the city remind me of the simple beauty I had fallen in love with all those months ago.

Now, I felt like I was in control of my own narrative. And Hiro was my anchor through the storm.

We explored Paris at our own pace, no agendas, no expectations. Hiro had struggled with his own journey too, torn between his art and the lure of commercial success. We found solace in our honesty, in the quiet moments where words weren't necessary.

One evening, as we sat on a park bench overlooking the city, Hiro turned to me.

"Amelia," he said softly, *"I know it hasn't been easy. But I think you've found something that most people never do, peace. You've found your center again."*

As I looked at him. *"I don't know if I've found all the answers,"* I whispered. *"But I think I'm finally asking the right questions."*

Over time, my decision to slow down proved to be the right one.

I started taking on projects that aligned with my values, working with non-profits and organizations that felt meaningful. The pressure to conform faded as I embraced a slower, more deliberate pace. To my surprise, my work began to resonate even more deeply with the people who saw it.

Through it all, Hiro stood by my side.

Our relationship deepened, not in grand gestures, but in the quiet understanding that we were both growing. And sometimes, that was all we needed.

In the end, I didn't have to choose between love and career. By embracing authenticity, I found that the two could coexist, not as opposing forces, but as parts of a greater whole.

Everything fell into place, with Hiro by my side. I realized that love too had its own rhythm, one that could harmonize perfectly with my ambitions.

Chapter 10

A New Direction

I had found peace in stepping away from the chaos of m former life. The fast-paced, high-pressure world I had once embraced felt like a distant memory. My days were slower, more intentional. I spent most of my time building my foundation, mentoring young photographers who shared my passion for authentic storytelling.

And yet, there was a quiet pull that lingered in the background, a faint whisper calling me back to the world of fashion photography. Only now, I saw it differently. It wasn't about fame or validation anymore. It was about using my voice, my lens, in a way that felt meaningful.

One afternoon, I sat in a quiet café in Paris, the soft hum of conversations blending with the clinking of coffee cups. My phone buzzed with a message from my manager. As I read it, my breath caught.

A renowned gallery in Milan was inviting me to host a solo exhibition. They wanted me to showcase my journey, a blend of my personal work and the stories I had captured along my travels.

It was the kind of opportunity that could reignite my career. The kind of opportunity of which I had once dreamed.

But now, it came with a new set of questions.

Was I ready to step back into the spotlight? Could I reenter that world without losing myself again?

I stared at the message, the invitation glowing on the screen, my thoughts swirling. Milan. A solo exhibition showcasing my journey.

Hiro sat across the table, quietly observing me. He had a way of sensing my emotions before I even spoke.

"Whatever you choose, it'll be the right decision," he said, his voice calm and steady. *"But just remember, this is your story, Amelia. You don't have to fit into anyone else's narrative."* His words settled my restless thoughts, like a puzzle piece clicking into place.

I looked up at him, my heart swelling with gratitude. *"Thank you,"* I said softly. *"For always reminding me of that."*

Hiro smiled, his eyes warm. *"It's easy when it's the truth."*

As we left the café and stepped into the Parisian streets, I thought about the offer, about the path that lay ahead. The idea of sharing my journey through a solo exhibition thrilled me, but it also terrified me.

This time, though, I wasn't making the decision out of fear or obligation. I felt like I had the space to decide what mattered to me.

Hiro's words echoed in my mind: *This is your story*. For so long I had let others write my narrative. But now, I was ready to take the pen back into my hands. This was my story. And I was finally ready to write the next chapter. After days of contemplation, I made my decision.

I would accept the invitation to Milan, but it had to be on my terms. This wasn't about chasing fame or money anymore; it was about creating something that felt authentic. Something that reflected who I was now, not who I had been.

For the first time in years, I felt a sense of control. I wasn't running to meet expectations or prove anything. I was building a space where my true self could finally shine.

I called my manager the next morning, my voice steady but excited.

"I'm doing this," I said firmly. *"But I'm doing it my way."*

Her relief and excitement on the other end of the line were unmistakable. *"That's exactly what we need,"* she said. *"Let's make it yours."*

The preparations for the exhibition were intense, but this time, I didn't feel the familiar weight of anxiety. Instead, I approached every decision with calm focus.

I spent hours sifting through my photographs, choosing each piece with care. This wasn't just an exhibition; it reflected my journey. I wanted every image to tell a story, to show not only the professional success I had achieved but also the personal growth that had shaped me.

The series began in Iceland, with its haunting stillness and stark landscapes. It moved through Italy, bursting with color and life, into India, where resilience shone through every frame. Then came Japan, its quiet harmony and deliberate beauty a mirror to my own search for balance.

I added a new series, a deeply personal one, that I had created since slowing down in Paris. The images were softer, quieter, focusing on small, fleeting moments, an elderly couple sharing a meal, children chasing pigeons, Hiro sketching by the Seine. They were pieces of my soul that I hadn't been ready to show before.

Each photograph was a chapter, a testament to the lessons I had learned and the beauty I had found in imperfection. This wasn't just a showcase of my work, it reflected the woman I had become.

This exhibition was a celebration of where I'd been, and an acknowledgment of where I was now.

Hiro was by my side through it all. He offered suggestions without overstepping, quietly encouraging me as I pieced together the story I wanted to tell. His presence grounded me, reminding me why I had fallen in love with photography in the first place.

"You're creating something beautiful," he said one evening as we reviewed the final layout. *"Not just with your photographs, but with how you're sharing them. It's honest, Amelia. It's you."*

His words echoed in my mind as the opening night drew closer.

I wasn't just curating an exhibition; I was reclaiming my narrative. And now, I felt ready to step into the light on my own terms.

Chapter 11

Milan and Me

Milan welcomed me with open arms.

The gallery was breathtaking, its lofty ceilings and soft, golden lighting casting a gentle glow over the photographs, creating the perfect stage for my work. The opening night felt like a dream, with artists, critics, and collectors from all over the world filling the space. They praised the collection, calling it *"a triumph of vulnerability and vision."*

And yet, as I stood there, surrounded by applause, I realized something: the validation wasn't what mattered anymore.

I had found fulfilment in the process itself, the quiet moments spent capturing a story, the hours piecing together a narrative that felt true. The applause was nice, but it wasn't the driving force behind my work anymore.

Hiro arrived in Milan a day after the exhibition opened, his presence grounding me in a way that no crowd or compliment ever could.

We spent our evenings exploring the city, wandering through galleries and tucked-away bookshops. Milan's art scene was alive, electric and it reminded both of us why we had fallen in love with creating in the first place.

One night, as we strolled along the Navigli canal, Hiro reached for my hand. His touch was steady and warm, and I couldn't help but smile as we walked beneath the soft glow of the streetlights.

"I'm proud of you," he said quietly, his voice carrying a weight that made me stop.

I turned to look at him, the reflection of the water dancing in his eyes.

"You've done something few people can do—you've stayed true to yourself," he continued.

A warmth spread through my chest. *"I've learned that authenticity is the most powerful thing we can offer the world,"* I said. *"And I'm grateful you've been here, supporting me through it all."*

We paused on a small bridge, the lights of the city shimmering on the canal below.

"Amelia," Hiro said, his voice softer now, almost hesitant. *"I've been thinking about our future. About how we can keep creating, together."*

My breath caught as I met his gaze. There was something in his expression, hope, maybe or the weight of something he hadn't yet said.

"What do you mean?" I asked gently, my heart pounding in anticipation.

Hiro smiled, his fingers tightening slightly around mine. *"I mean us. I mean building something, together. You've created a life that's so honest and full of meaning. I want to be part of that. Not just here and there, but... always."*

His words settled into me like the final note of a melody I'd always known but had been waiting to hear.

I took a deep breath, my mind racing with everything we'd been through, the roads we had walked separately and together. Every argument, every reconciliation, every quiet moment had brought us here, to this bridge beneath the lights of Milan, where everything finally felt aligned.

In the weeks following the exhibition, my career soared to heights I hadn't predicted. Invitations poured in, from galleries across Europe, from conference organizers asking me to speak about the importance of authentic storytelling in an increasingly digital world. My photographs weren't just being seen; they were being felt.

Critics praised the technical skill in my work, but it wasn't the sharpness of the image or the precision of the composition they talked about. It was the heart and soul behind every frame. They called it *"transformative,"* but to me, it simply felt honest.

As my career blossomed, I found myself drawn more deeply to the purpose that had carried me through the toughest moments of my journey: inspiring and uplifting others.

I began taking on projects that focused on social issues, using my platform to shine a light on the stories too often ignored. There was power in using my lens to amplify marginalized voices, to bring visibility to the invisible.

It wasn't about me; it was about the people in the photographs, about giving them the dignity and recognition they deserved.

With Hiro by my side, it felt easy.

Our bond had grown into something more than personal, it had become a partnership in every sense of the word. Together, we embarked on joint projects that blended our creative visions. His architectural designs and my photography told stories in tandem, creating spaces where art and advocacy intersected.

Our work wasn't just about beauty; it was about impact.

We designed installations that highlighted the resilience of communities rebuilding after disaster. We created exhibitions that brought together voices from diverse cultures, weaving a tapestry of shared humanity.

Hiro's quiet strength and unwavering support became my foundation. His belief in me never wavered, even when I doubted myself. And in return, I found myself cheering him on, encouraging him to explore the bold, uncharted ideas that had always lingered in the corners of his mind.

One evening, as we reviewed a proposal for a joint project, a community center designed to showcase local artists while providing resources for underserved creatives, I realized how far we had come.

I looked at Hiro, his face lit by the soft glow of his laptop screen and felt a wave of gratitude.

"We're doing something real," I said, breaking the silence.

He glanced up, his expression thoughtful. *"We always were,"* he said simply.

I smiled, leaning back in my chair. For the first time in years, I wasn't chasing something just out of reach. I wasn't seeking approval or trying to outrun my doubts. I was creating, connecting, and growing, not just as an artist, but as myself.

I was exactly where I needed to be.

Chapter 12

The Proposal

The years had been kind to us.

Hiro and I had built a life together, one filled with love, creativity, and an unwavering respect for each other's dreams. We had shared so much, the triumphs, the challenges, the quiet nights spent working side by side.

And yet, nothing could have prepared me for that evening in Tokyo.

We were sitting on the rooftop of a small building in the heart of the city, the sky painted in shades of orange and pink as the sun dipped below the skyline. The air was cool, carrying the faint hum of the city below. I leaned into Hiro, savoring the peaceful rhythm of the moment.

But then he shifted, turning to face me. There was a seriousness in his expression that made my heart skip.

"I've been thinking," he began, taking my hand in his. His voice was steady, but his grip was just tight enough to betray his nerves. *"About all the moments that have brought us here. The travels, the challenges, the quiet nights... and I've realized that I want to spend the rest of my life with you."*

The world seemed to stop.

"Hiro..." I whispered, my chest tightening with emotion.

He held my gaze, his dark eyes steady and filled with something unshakable. *"I know we've both been through a lot,"* he continued, his voice soft but certain. *"But I believe in us. In what we've built together. So, Amelia... will you marry me?"*

Tears welled up in my eyes as his words sank in. I thought of everything we had shared, the long walks in Paris, the creative projects that had shaped our careers, the moments of doubt when we had held each other steady.

As Hiro's words settled over me, I felt the weight of every moment that had brought us here. This wasn't just a proposal. It was a promise, it was a culmination of everything we had built together.

"Yes," I said, my voice breaking as I threw my arms around him. *"Yes, a thousand times yes."*

We stayed there, wrapped in each other's arms as the city lights twinkled around us, their soft glow marking the start of a new chapter.

In that moment, I knew that whatever lay ahead, new challenges, new adventures, new stories to tell, we would face it together.

This was the life we had built, and this was the love we had found. And I couldn't wait to see where it would take us next.

our wedding was simple, just as we'd envisioned.

It was held in a small garden in Paris, tucked away from the city's bustle. The late afternoon light spilled over the ivy-covered walls, casting everything in a warm, golden glow. It wasn't a grand event, no elaborate floral displays or massive guest list. Instead, it was intimate and honest, much like the love Hiro and I had built.

Close friends, family, and the people who had supported us throughout our journey stood around us as we exchanged vows.

"I promise to grow with you," Hiro said, his voice steady but filled with emotion, *"to honor the person you are and the person you're becoming."*

The golden light of the Parisian afternoon wrapped around us as we stood hand in hand. I felt the weight of Hiro's words, each one a thread weaving our lives together.

"And I promise to do the same," I replied, tears threatening to spill of overwhelming joy. *"To walk beside you, not just as your partner, but as someone who will always believe in you."*

As we slipped the rings onto each other's fingers, I felt a profound sense of calm, as though the world had finally clicked into place.

In the years that followed, life unfolded in ways I could have never imagined.

I continued to thrive in my career, finding a balance between my work and personal life that once felt impossible. My photographs remained influential, but it was the work of the artists I mentored that truly inspired me.

Through the foundation Hiro and I nurtured together, we offered scholarships and mentorships to young photographers from around the world. Watching them grow and create reminded me of why I'd started this journey in the first place.

Through it all, Hiro was my anchor.

He was the one who could always see me clearly, even when I couldn't see myself. Together, we traveled the world, not chasing after something, but simply exploring, creating, and living in a way that felt true to who we were.

I captured fleeting moments with my camera, while Hiro sketched or studied the architecture of the places we visited. Our work often intertwined, his designs shaped by the stories I captured, my photographs inspired by his eye for structure and form.

In every corner of the world, we found beauty, not just in the places we visited, but in the act of experiencing them together.

There was a time when I felt lost, unsure of who I was or where I was going. But through the struggles, the love and the quiet moments of reflection, I discovered that the journey mattered as much as the destination.

Now, at last, I was exactly where I was meant to be, living a life full of meaning, connection, and love.

And as I looked at Hiro one quiet evening, as we sat together under the stars, I realized that the greatest gift of all wasn't just the life we had built.

It was the fact that we had built it together.

Years after the exhibition in Milan, my life was transformed in ways I never could have imagined when I first set out on my journey.

What began as a pursuit of fame and recognition had evolved into something far deeper: an exploration of the world through my lens, capturing moments that truly mattered. The stories I told weren't just mine, they belonged to people whose voices had often been overlooked, whose resilience had inspired me in ways I hadn't expected.

My name was no longer just associated with fashion. The work I was known for now had meaning, weight. Each photograph I took felt like a piece of a larger puzzle, one that wasn't about recognition but about creating a legacy of authenticity and purpose.

The foundation we had nurtured over the years became one of our proudest accomplishments. We created not just opportunities but communities, safe spaces for young talents.

Through mentorship programs and scholarships, I watched young photographers from every corner of the world step into their own, finding their voices in a world that often tried to drown them out.

I spent my days leading workshops, listening to their stories and sharing the wisdom I had gained through my own struggles. There was something profoundly humbling about watching someone else's journey unfold, knowing I had played even a small role in helping them along the way.

Hiro had become more than my partner. He was my anchor, my collaborator, my mirror.

We had grown together in ways I never thought possible, blending our creative talents into projects that transcended borders and cultures. Our work wasn't just about art anymore; it was about impact.

We traveled the world together, creating installations and exhibitions that told stories of resilience, hope and humanity. Hiro understood me in a way no one else ever had. He didn't just support my dreams, he shared them. And I did the same for him.

Our life in Paris was a peaceful one.

Mornings often began quietly, with coffee on the balcony as the city came to life around us. Some days we would dive into creative brainstorming sessions that stretched into the evening. Other times, we'd pack our bags and take spontaneous trips to explore new places.

I no longer felt the need to fill the silences with answers to my questions. I had learned to embrace the uncertainty, to trust in the unfolding of the journey. Life, I realized, didn't need to be controlled, it needed to be lived.

What I once thought was a path to external success had transformed into something far more fulfilling.

True success wasn't in the applause or the accolades; it was in staying true to myself. It was in helping others find their voices, in building a life that was rich with love, creativity and purpose.

Looking back, I could see how every twist and turn, every moment of doubt and discovery, had shaped me into who I was today. Each frame I captured, each story I told, had been a piece of the larger puzzle, a journey not toward fame, but toward wholeness.

I had found peace, not in the world's applause, but in the quiet contentment of knowing I had created a life that was uniquely mine. One filled with passion, love and an ever-evolving story.

And as I stood on the balcony one evening, watching the Paris skyline light up, I felt a deep sense of gratitude for the journey that had led me here.

The End.